I0611610

Dionyse Settle, Abraham Fleming

A true reporte of the laste voyage into the west and northwest

regions

Dionyse Settle, Abraham Fleming

A true reporte of the laste voyage into the west and northwest regions

ISBN/EAN: 9783742830968

Manufactured in Europe, USA, Canada, Australia, Japa

Cover: Foto ©Andreas Hilbeck / pixelio.de

Manufactured and distributed by brebook publishing software
(www.brebook.com)

Dionyse Settle, Abraham Fleming

A true reporte of the laste voyage into the west and northwest

regions

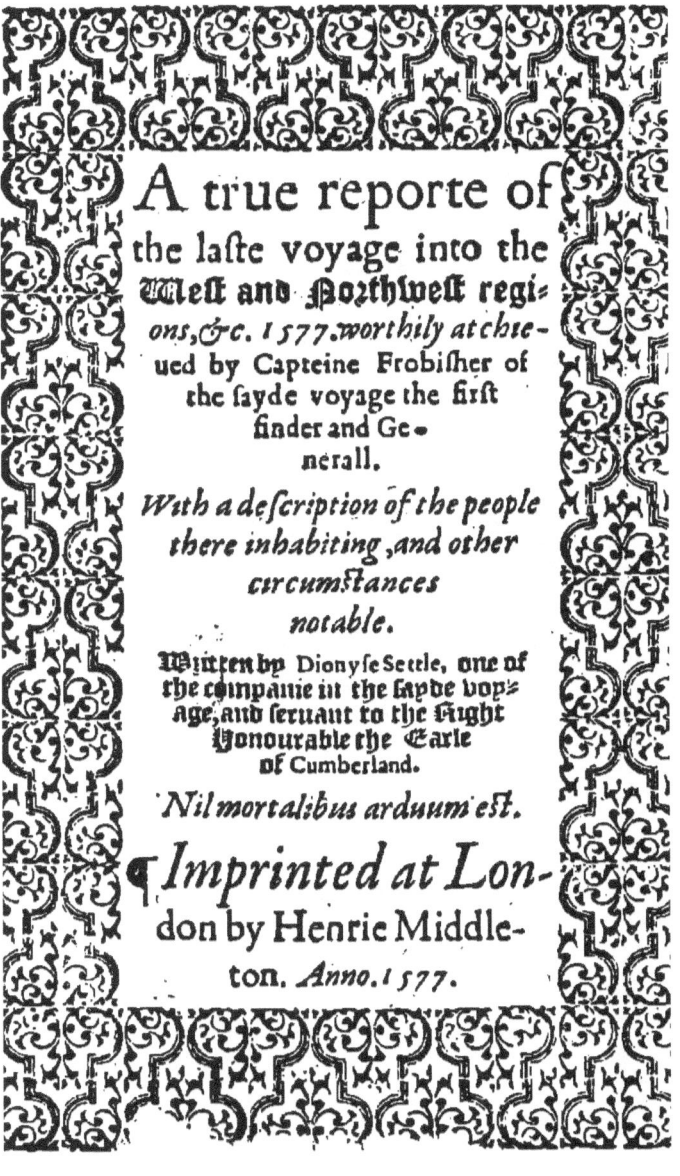

A true reporte of
the laste voyage into the
West and Northwest regi=
ons, &c. 1577. worthily at chie-
ued by Capteine Frobisher of
the sayde voyage the first
finder and Ge-
nerall.

With a description of the people
there inhabiting, and other
circumstances
notable.

Written by Dionyse Settle, one of
the companie in the sayde voy=
age, and seruant to the Right
Honourable the Earle
of Cumberland.

Nil mortalibus arduum est.

❡ Imprinted at Lon-
don by Henrie Middle-
ton. Anno. 1577.

JOHN CARTER BROWN

A RYTHME DECASYLLABI-
call, vpon this last luckie voyage of worthie
Capteine Frobisher. 1577.

John Carter Brown
Library

THrough sundrie foming fretes, and storming streightes,
That ventrous knight of Ithac' soyle did saile :
Againſt the force of Syrens baulmed beightes,
His noble ſkill and courage did preuaile.
His hap was hard, his hope yet nothing fraile.
　Not ragged Rockes, not ſinking Syrtes or ſands
　His ſtoutneſſe ſtaide, from viewing forreigne lands.

That Poets penne and paines was well employd,
His braines bedeawd with dropps of Parnaſſe ſpring :
Whereby renowne deſerued he enioyd.
Yea, nowe (though dead) the Muſes ſweetly ſing,
Melodiouſly by note, and tuned ſtring,
　They found in th'eares of people farre and neere,
　Th'exceeding praiſe of that approued Peere.

A right Heroicall heart of Britanne blood,
Vlyſſes match in ſkill and Martiall might :
For Princes fame, and countries ſpeciall good,
Through brackiſh ſeas (where Neptune reignes by right)
Hath ſafely ſaild, in perils great deſpight :
　The Golden fleece (like Iaſon) hath he got,
　And rich returnd, ſaunce loſſe or luckleſſe lot.

O that I had old Homers worthy witt,
O that I had, this preſent houre, his head :
With penne in hand, then muſing would I ſitt,
And our Vlyſſes valiant venture ſpread
In vaunting verſe, that when his corps is dead,
　(Which long may liue) his true renowne may reſt,
　As one whome God aboundantly hath bleſt.

Abraham Fleming.

¶ To the Right honourable

and my singular good Lord, George Earle of
Cumberland, Baron Clifford, Lord of Skipton and
Veſſcie : his humble ſeruaunt Dionyſe Settle,
wiſheth the fulneſſe of all
perfect felicitie.

*T both is, and hath beene, (Right
Honourable)the bountie of a noble
mynde, not to expect remuneration
or ſatiſſaction for liberalitie frankly
beſtowed. It both is, and alſo hath
beene accounted a great vice, to ſeeme vnthank-
full, or at the leaſt not ſomthing carefull, of whom,
when, and how, we ſhould receiue liberalitie. I am
not obliuious, neither careleſſe, when, and how, your
Honour(aboue my expectation)nobly ſatiſſied the
requeſt of me your humble ſeruant. I am moſt aſ-
ſured, that the vertue of your noble heart expec-
teth nothing of me, but that your goodneſſe might
abound to my profite : vppon which occaſion, and
bicauſe I would not be accounted ingratefull, I
haue both boldly paſſed the limittes of my duetie,
and alſo vnlearnedly taken vpon me to ſet foorth
ſome thing worthie notice, in this laſt voyage of
our Capteine and Generall, Maiſter Martine
Frobiſher, your Honours worthie Countrie man :
vnder whome (as your Honours vnworthie ſeruant)I was one in the ſaid voyage. By his great diligence, the voyage is worthily finiſhed: whereby*

A.ij.   *I am*

I am perſuaded, that he will refell the rehearſall of
thoſe opprobrious wordes, namely, that, All euill
cōmeth from or hath originall in the North:
not onely he, but many worthie ſubiectes more.

I haue publiſhed this ſcantling, vnder the noble title of your Honor, to whom I offer the ſame in
dedication: which, though it be not decorated with
good learning, apte for the ſetting foorth of ſo notable a matter: yet, the ſame is beautified with
good will and trueth. Wherein your Honour, (if
it ſhall ſo pleaſe you) for recreation ſake, may vn-
derſtand, what people, countries, and other commodities we haue found out, ſince our departure
from England, which haue not ben knowne before.
Thus, preſuming vpon hope and aſſuraunce of your
Honours pardon for my bolde attempt herein, I
reſt humbly at your Lordſhips commaundement:
wiſhing your time ſo ſpent in this world, that
you may inioy the felicitie in the
worlde to come.
Amen.

Your Lorpſhips moſt hum-
ble ſeruaunt to commaund,

John Carter Brown
Library

Dionyſe Settle.

To the Christian
Reader.

John Carter Brown Library

Vch countries and people,
(good Chriſtian Reader)
which almoſt from the de-
luge, or at the leaſt, ſo long
as anye humane creature
hath had habitation on the earth, haue of
late yeres, by ÿ induſtrie of diligent ſear-
chers ben explored: it hath likewiſe pleaſed God, ÿ they ſhould be found out by
thoſe people, which for the temperature
of their habitatiõ, are moſt apt to atchiue
the ſame. As for example, the Spaniards,
the Weſt Indies. Spaine is ſituated much
more neere ÿ Tropike of Cancer, then o-
ther Chriſtian countries be: wherby, the
Spaniards are better able to tolerate Phœ-
bus burning beames, then others whiche
are more Septentrional thẽ they. Wherfore, I ſuppoſe them the moſt apte men
for the inioying of the habitation of the
Weſt Indies: and eſpecially ſo much, as
is vexed with continual heate, or that is a-
greeable to their temperature, God hath

A.iii.   bene

ben pleaſed that they,as the moſt apt people, ſhould both explore & inioy ẏ ſame.
Semblably, ẏ Portugals,whoſe temperature is correſpondent to ẏ Spaniards,God
is alſo contented,that they haue explored
Africa, euen through the burning Zone,
both the Weſt and South coaſt,with al ẏ
coaſt of Aſia,vnto the Oriental cape therof, and the Iſlands adiacent to them both:
wherefore, both for their habitation, and
temperature, I account them ẏ moſt apt
people to atchiue ẏ ſame, and to reape the
benefite, where about they haue taken no
ſmall paines and labor. In like maner,the
French men, where ẏ Spaniards thought
ẏ place not apt for their temperature, diſ-
couered Noua Francia, and other places
in America:wherfore,I iudge them worthie the commoditie thereof, as people
moſt apt to inioy and poſſeſſe the ſame.
Laſtly,it hath pleſed God,at this preſent,
by the great diligence & care of our worthie Countrieman,Maſter Martine Frobiſher, in the 18. and 19. yeare of oure
Queenes Maieſties reigne, to diſcouer,
for

for the vtilitie of his Prince and Countrie, other regions more Septentrional,
then thoſe before rehearſed : which, from
the beginning, as vnknowne till nowe,
haue bene concealed and hidden. Which
diſcouerie, I iudge moſt apt for vs Engliſh
men, and more agreeing to our temperature, then others aboue rehearſed. I leaue
the famous diſcouerie of Moſcouie, and
other countries on thoſe partes, (whiche
of late yeares haue bene explored by the
induſtrie of other our worthie countri-
men)to the diligent Reader: whereby he
may conſider, that this our countrie, hath
foſtered vp men of no leſſe value and ex-
cellencie, then thoſe, which are intituled,
The ſecond, thirde, and fourth Neptune.
And doubtleſſe, hee, by whoſe endeuour
this laſt diſcouerie of the world is explored, may bee celebrated as well with the
title of Aeolus, as alſo of Neptune. By
whoſe ſingular knowledge and cunning,
God hath preſerued vs in this voyage,
from bothe their cruell daungers.

Thus(Chriſtiã Reader) thou maiſt perceiue, that the worlde, of late yeares, hath beene difcouered by fundrie regions of this our Europe : which God hath fo diuided in the exploring of the fame, that it feemeth apt and agreeable to the difcouerer, more then to any other, to inioy all fuch commodities as they yealde and affoorde. Confider alfo, that Chriftians haue difcouered thefe countries and people, which fo long haue lyen vnknowne, and they not vs : which plainely may argue, that it is Gods good will and pleafure, that they fhould be inftructed in his diuine feruice and religion, whiche from the beginning, haue beene nouzeled and nourifhed in Atheifme, groffe ignorance, and barbarous behauiour. Wherefore, this is my iudgement, (in conclufion) that who fo euer can winne them from their infidelitie, to the perfect knowledge of his diuine inftitutions and feruice, hee or they are worthie to receiue the greateft rewarde at Gods hands, and the greater benefites from thofe countries, which he hath difcouered. Fare well.

¶A true report of Cap-
teine Frobisher his laſt voyage into
the Weſt, and Northweſt regions,
this preſent yere 1577. With
a deſcription of the people
there inhabiting.

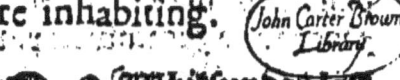
John Carter Brown Library

On Whitſunday laſt
paſt, being the 26. of
May, in this preſent
yeare of our Lorde
God 1577. Capteine
Frobiſher departed
from Blacke Wall,
with one of the Queenes Maieſties
ſhippes, called The Aide, of nine ſcore
tunne, or there aboutes: and two other
little Barkes likewiſe, the one called
The Gabriel, whereof Maiſter Fenton
a Gentleman of my Lord of Warwicks
was Capteine: and the other, The Mi-
chael, whereof Maiſter Yorke a Gentleman of my Lorde Admerals was Cap-
tein, accompanied with ſeuen ſcore gentlemen, ſouldiers and ſaylers, well fur-

B.   niſhed

nished with victuals, and other prouisō
necessarie for one halfe yere, on this his
seconde voyage, for the further discoue-
ring of the passage to Cataia, and other
countries thereunto adiacent, by West
and Northwest Nauigations : whiche
passage, or way, is supposed to be on the
North and Northwest partes of America : and the sayd America to be an Islande inuironed with the sea, where-
through our Merchaunts might haue
course and recourse with their mer-
chandize, from these our Northernmost
parts of Europe, to those oriental coasts
of Asia, in much shorter time, and with
greater benefit then any others, to their
no little commoditie and profite that
doe traffique the same. Oure sayde
Capteine and Generall of this present
voyage and companie, hauing the yere
before, with two little Pinnisses, to
his great daunger and no small com-
mendations, giuen a worthy attempt
towardes the performaunce thereof, is
also prest (when occasion shall be mini-
stred, to the benefite of his Prince and
natiue countrie) to aduenture him selfe
further

of Capteine Frobisher.

further therein. As for this second voyage, it seemeth sufficient, that he hath better explored and searched the commodities of those people and countries, with sufficient commoditie vnto the aduenturers, which in his first voyage the yeare before he had found out.

Upon which considerations, the day and yeare before expressed, we departed from Blacke Wall to Harwiche, where making an accomplishment of thinges necessarie, the last of Maye we hoysed vp sailes, and with a mery winde the 7. therof we arriued at the Ilands called Orchades, or vulgarly Orkney, being in number 30. subiect and adiacent to Scotland, where we made prouision of freshe water : in the doing whereof, our Generall licenced the Gentlemen and Souldiers, for their recreation, to go on shoare. At our landing, the people fled from their poore cotages, with shrikes and alarums, to warne their neighbors of enimies : but by gentle persuasions we reclaimed them to their houses . It seemeth they are often frighted with Pirates, or some other enimies, that moueth

B.ij.   ueth

ueth them to such souden feare. Their
houses are very simplie builded with
pibble stone, without any chimneys, the
fire being made in the middest thereof.
The good man, wife, children, and other
of their familie, eate and sléepe on the
one side of the house, and their cattell on
the other, very beastly and rudely, in respect of ciuilitie. They are destitute of
wood , their fire is turffes and Cowe
shardes . They haue corne, bigge ,
and oates, with whiche they paye their
Kinges rente, to the maintenance of
his house. They take great quantitie of
fishe , which they drie in the winde and
Sunne. They dresse their meate very
filthily, and eate it without salt. Their
apparell is after the rudest sort of Scotland. Their money is all base . Their
churche and religion is reformed accor-
ding to the Scots. The fisher men of
England, can better declare the dispost-
tions of those people than I : wherfore,
I remit other their vsages to their re-
portes, as yearely repairers thither, in
their course to and from Island for fish.

of Capteine Frobisher.

Wée departed herehence, the 8. of June, and followed our course betwéene West and Northwest, vntill the 4. of Julie: all which time, we had no night, but that easily, and without any impediment, we had when we were so dispoſed, the fruition of our bookes, and other pleaſures to paſſe awaye the time: a thinge of no small moment, to such as wander in vnknowen seas and longe Nauigations, eſpecially, when both the winds, and raging surges, do paſſe their common and wonted course. This benefite endureth in thoſe partes not ſirs wéekes, whileſt the Sunne is néere the Tropike of Cancer: but where the Pole is raiſed to 70. or 80. degrées, it continueth the longer.

All along theſe seas, after we were 6. dayes ſayling from Orkney, we met floting in the sea, great Firre trées, which as wée iudged, were with the furie of great floudes rooted vp, and so driuen into the sea. Iſland hath almoſt no other wood nor fewel, but such as they take vp vpon their coaſtes. It ſéemeth, that theſe trées are driuen from some parte of the New found land, with the Current that setteth from the Weſt to the Eaſt.

The 4. of Julie, we came within the making of Freeseland. From this ſhoare 10. or 12. leagues, we met great Iſlandꝰ of yce, of halfe a mile, some moꝛe, somꝰ leſſe in compaſſe, ſhewing aboue the sea 30. oꝛ 40. fathomes, and as we suppoſed, faſt on ground, where, with oure leade wée could scarse found the bottome foꝛ deapth.

Here, in place of odoꝛiferous and fragrant smelles of swéete gummes, and pleasant notes of muſicall birdes, which other Countries in moꝛe temperate Zone do yéeld, we taſted the moſt boiſteꝛous Boreall blaſts, mirt with snow and haile, in the moneth of June and Julie, nothing inferiour to oure vntemperate Winter: a soudeine alteration, and eſpecially in a place oꝛ Paralele, where the Pole is not eleuate aboue 61. degrées: at which height other countries moꝛe to the Noꝛth, yea, vnto 70. degrées, ſhewe théselues moꝛe temperat than this doth.

All

(marginal notes:)
ceſland,

andes of
c.

e, snowe,
d haile in
ne and Ju-

# of Capteine Frobisher.

All along this coast yce lyeth, as a continuall bullwoꝛke, and so defendeth the countrie, that those whiche woulð land there incurre great daunger. Our Generall thꝛée dayes together, attempted with the shippboate to haue gone on shoaꝛe, whiche, foꝛ that without great daunger he coulð not accomplishe, he deferred it vntil a moꝛe conuenient time. All along the coast lye very highe mounteines couered with snowe, excepte in such places, where, thꝛough the stǽpenesse of the mounteines, of foꝛce it must nǽdes fall.

Foure dayes coastinge along this Land, we found no signe of habitation. Little birdes, whiche we iudged to haue lost ỹ shoare, by reason of thicke fogges, whiche that countrie is much subiect vnto, came fléeing to oure shippes, whiche causeth vs to suppose, that the countrie is both moꝛe tollerable, and also habitable within, then the outward shoare maketh shewe oꝛ signification.

From hence we departed the eight of Julie: and the 16. of the same, we came

B. iiij.   within

Yce defendeth Freeland.

The shoare Freeland highe mounteines.

Freeland subiect to foggs

Little birdes signe and token of habitation.

within the making of land, whiche land
our Generall, the yeare before, had named The Queenes foreland: being an
Iland, as we iudge, lying néere the ſuppoſed continent with America: & on the
other ſide, oppoſite to ÿ ſame, one other
Iland called Halles Iſle, after the name
of the Maiſter of our ſhippe; néere adiacent to the firme land, ſuppoſed continent with Aſia. Betwéene the which
two Ilandes, there is a large entrance
oɾ ſtreight, called Frobiſhers ſtreight, after the name of oure Generall, the firſt
finder thereof. This ſaid ſtreight, is
ſuppoſed to haue paſſage into the Sea of
Sur, which I leaue vnknowne as yet.

It ſéemeth, that either here, oɾ not
farre hence, the Sea ſhould haue moɾe
large entraunce, than in other partes,
within the froſen oɾ vntemperate Zone:
and that ſome contrarie tide, either from
the Eaſt oɾ Weſt, with maine foɾce ca-
ſteth out that great quantitie of yce,
which commeth floating from this coaſt,
euen vnto Freeſland, cauſing that countrie to ſéeme moɾe vntemperate than o-
thers,

thers ; muche more Northerly than
they are.

I cannot iudge, that any temperature vnder the Pole, beeing the time of
the Sunnes Northerne declination,
halfe a yeare together and one whole
day, (considering, that the Sunnes cleuation surmounteth not 23. degrees and
30. minutes,) can haue power to dissolue
such monstruous and huge yce, comparable to great mounteines, excepte by
some other force, as by swift Currents
and tydes, with the helpe of the said day
of halfe a yeare.

Before we came within the making
of these Landes, we tasted cold stormes,
insomuch that it seemed, we had chaunged Summer with winter, if the length
of the dayes had not remoued vs from
that opinion.

At our first comming, the streightes
seemed to be shutt vp with a long mure
of yce, whiche gaue no little cause of discomfort vnto vs all : but our Generall,
(to whose diligence, imminent daungers, and difficult attemptes seemed nothing,

B.v.

Islands of
comparable
mounteine

Capteine F
bisher his f
ciall care a

thing, in reſpect of his willing mind, for
the commoditie of his Prince and countrie,) with two little Pinniſes prepa-
red of purpoſe, paſſed twiſe thorough
them to the Eaſt ſhoare, and the Iſlands
therevnto adiacent: and the ſhippe, with
the two barks, lay off and on ſomething
further into the ſea, from the daunger of
the yce.

he order of
e people ap-
aring on
oare.

      Whileſt he was ſearching the coun-
trie néere the ſhoare, ſome of the people
of the countrie ſhewed themſelues, lea-
ping and dauncing, with ſtraunge ſhri-
kes and cryes, whiche gaue no little ad-
miration to our men. Our Generall de-
ſtrous to allure them vnto him by faire
meanes, cauſed kniues, & other thinges,
to be proferred vnto them, whiche they
would not take at our handes: but béeing layd on the ground, & the partie go-
ing away, they came and tooke vp, leauing ſomething of theirs to counter-
uaile ſ ſame. At the length, two of them
leauing their weapons, came downe to
our Generall and Maiſter, who did the
like to them, commaunding the compa-
                       nie to

nie to ſtay, and went vnto them : who,
after certeine dumbe ſignes and mute
congratulations, began to lay handes
vpon them, but they deliuerly eſcaped, Fierce and
and ranne to their bowes and arrowes, bould peop
and came fiercely vppon them, (not re-
ſpecting the reſt of our companie, which
were readie foʒ their defence) but with
their arrowes hurt diuerſe of them : we One taken.
tooke the one, and the other eſcaped.

　Whileſt our Generall was buſied in
ſearching the countrie and thoſe Jſlands
adiacent on the Eaſt ſhoare, the ſhip and
barckes hauing great care, not to put
farre into the ſea from him, foʒ that he
had ſmall ſtoʒe of bictuals, were foʒced
to abide in a cruell tempeſt, chancing in
the night, amongſt and in the thickeſt of
the yce, which was ſo monſtruous, that
euen the leaſt of a thouſand had béene of
foʒce ſufficient, to haue ſhiuered oure
ſhippe and barkes into ſmall poʒtions,
if God (who in all neceſſities, hath care
vpon the infirmitie of man) had not pʒo-
uided foʒ this our extremitie a ſufficient
remedie, thʒough the light of the night,
　　　　　　　　　　　　　whereby

whereby we might well diſcerne to fliē from ſuch imminent daungers, whiche wēe auoyded with 14. Bourdes in one watch the ſpace of 4. houres. If we had not incurred this danger amongſt theſe monſtrous Iſlandes of yce, wēe ſhould haue loſt our Generall and Maiſter, and the moſt of our beſt ſailers, which were on the ſhoare deſtitute of victualls: but rd Coxe by the valure of our Maiſter Gunner, er Gun- being expert both in Nauigation and o-ther good qualities, we were all content to incurre the dangers afore rehearſed, before we would, with oure owne ſafe-tie, runne into the Seas, to the deſtru-ction of oure ſaid Generall and his com-panie.

The day following, being the 19. of Julie, oure Capteine returned to the ſhippe, with good newes of great riches, which ſhewed it ſelfe in the bowelles of thoſe barren mounteines, wherewith we were all ſatiffied. A ſouden mutati-on. The one parte of vs being almoſt ſwallowed vp the night before, wᵗ cruell Neptunes force, and the reſt on ſhoare,

takitg

of Capteine Frobisher.

taking thought foz their græbie paun=
ches,how to finb the way to New found New found land.
land : at one moment we were all rapt
with ioye, fozgetting, both where we
were,and what we hab suffred. Behold
the glozie of man, to night contemning
riches,and rather looking foz beath than
otherwise : and to mozrowe beuiſing
howe to ſatiſſie his græbie appetite
with Golbe.

Within foure days after we had ben
at the entraunce of the Streightes, the
Pozthwelt and Welt winbes diſperſed
the yce into the Sea, and mabe bs a
large entrance into the Streights, that
without any impebiment, on the 19. of
Julie, we entred them, and the 20, ther=
of oure Generall aud Maiſter, with
great diligence, ſought out and ſounded
the Welt ſhoare, and found out a fayze
Warbozough foz the ſhip and barkes to
ride in, and named it after our Maiſters
mate, Iackmans ſound, and bzought Iackmans ſound.
the ſhip, barkes, and all their companie
to ſafe anchoz, ercept one man, whiche
byed by Gods viſitation.

Who

Who so maketh Nauigations to these contries, hath not only extreme windes, and furious Seas, to encounter withall, but also many monstrous and great Ilandes of yce: a thing both rare, wonderfull, and greatly to be regarded.

We were forced, sundrie times, while the ship did ride here at anchor, to haue continuall watch, with boates and men readie with Hatsers, to knit fast vnto such yce, which with the ebbe and floud were tossed to and fro in the Harboroughe, and with force of oares to hale them away, for indaungering the ship.

Our Generall, certeine dayes searched this supposed continent with America, and not finding the commoditie to aunswere his expectation, after he had made tryall thereof, he departed thence with two little barkes, and men sufficient, to the East shoare, being the supposed continent of Asia, & left the ship with most of the Gentlemen, Souldiers, and Saylers, vntill such time as he, eyther thought good to send, or come for them.

The stones of this supposed continent

Marginal notes:
ce needefull be regarded seafaring en.

eat watche ith men and ates for yce daungering e ship at an- or.

of Capteine Frobisher.

nent with America, be altogether spark-
led, and glister in the Sunne like Gold:
so likewise doth the sande in the bright
water, yet they verifie the olde Prouerbe : All is not golde that glistereth.

Stones glist
with sparck
like Golde.

A common
Prouerbe.

On this West shoare we found a dead
fishe floating, whiche had in his nose a
horne streight & torquet, of lengthe two
yardes lacking two ynches, being bro-
ken in the top, where we might perceiue
it hollowe, into which some of our Saylers putting Spiders, they presently
dyed. I sawe not the tryall hereof, but it
was reported vnto me of a trueth : by
the vertue whereof, we supposed it to be
the sea Unicorne.

The Sea Vn-
corne.

After our Generall had founde out
good harborough for the Ship and Barkes to anchor in : and also suche store of
Golde oare as he thought him selfe sa-
tiffied withall, he sent backe oure Mai-
ster with one of the Barkes, to conducte
the great Ship vnto him, who coasting
along the West shoare, perceiued a
faire harborough, and willing to sound
the same, at the enterance thereof they
                                    espyed

elpped two tentes of Seale skinnes.

At the ſight of oure men, the people fled into the mounteines: neuertheleſſe, our ſayde Maiſter went to their tents, and left ſome of our trifles, as kniues, Bels, and Glaſſes, and departed, not taking any thing of theirs, excepte one Dogge to our Shippe.

On the ſame day, after conſultation had, we determined to ſee, if by fayre meanes we could eyther allure them to familiaritie, or otherwiſe take ſome of them, and ſo atteine to ſome knowlege of thoſe men, whome our Generall loſt the yeare before.

craftie peo-
e.

At our comming backe againe, to the place where their tentes were before, they had remoued their tentes further into the ſaid Bay or Sound, where they might, if they were driuen from the land, flee with their boates into the ſea. We parting our ſelues into two companies, and rompaſſing a mounteine, came ſoudeinly vppon them by land, who eſpying vs, without any tarying fled to their boates, leauing the moſt

part

part of their oares behind them for haſt,
and rowed downe the Bay, where our
two Pinniſſes met them, & droue them
to ſhoare: but, if they had had all their
oares, ſo ſwift are they in rowing, it had
bene loſt time to haue chafed them.

When they were landed, they fierce‐ A fierce aſ‐
ſault of a few
ly aſſaulted oure men with their bowes
and arrowes, who wounded three of
them with our arrowes: and percey‐
uing themſelues thus hurt, they deſpe‐ Deſperate
people.
rately leapt off the Rocks into the Sea,
and drowned themſelues: which if they
had not done, but had ſubmitted them
ſelues: or if by any meanes we could
haue taken them aliue, (being their
enimies as they iudged) we would both
haue ſaued them, and alſo haue ſought
remedie to cure their woundes receiued
at our handes. But they, altogether
voyde of humanitie, and ignorant what Ignoraunt
what merci
meaneth,
mercy meaneth, in extremities looke for
no other then death: and perceiuing
they ſhould fall into our handes, thus mi‐
ſerably by drowning rather deſired
death, then otherwiſe to be ſaued by vs:

C.   the

the reſt, perceiuing their fellowes in this diſtreſſe, fled into the highe moun-teines. Two women, not being ſo apt to eſcape as the men were, the one for her age, and the other being incombred with a yong childe, we toke. The olde wzetch, whome diuers of oure Saylers ſuppoſed to be eyther a Diuell, oz a Witche, plucked off her buſkins, to ſe, if ſhe were clouen foted, and foz her ougly hewe and deformitie, we let her goe : the young woman and the childe, we bzought away. We named the place where they were ſtayne, Bloudie point: and the Bay oz Harbozough, Yorkes ſound, after the name of one of the Cap-teines of the two Barkes.

Hauing this knowledge, both of their fierceneſſe and crueltie, and perceiuing that fayze meanes, as yet, is not able to allure them to familiaritie, we diſpoſed our ſelues, contrarie to our inclination, ſomething to be cruel, returned to their tentes, and made a ſpoyle of the ſame. Their riches are neyther Gold, Siluer, oz pzecious Dzaperie, but their ſayde

tentes

(marginal notes:)
ro women en and a lde.

olde wo-n a ſuppo-Diuell or itch.

udie nt. rks found.

re meanes able to al-e them to niliaritie.

tentes and boates, made of the skinnes Boates of skinnes.
of red Deare and Seale skinnes: also,
Dogges like vnto Wolues, but for the
most part black, with other trifles, more
to be wondred at for their strangenesse,
then for any other commoditie nædeful
for our vse.

Thus returning to our Ship, the 3. Oure departure from the West shoare.
of August, we departed from the West
shoare, supposed firme with America,
after we had anchored there 13. dayes:
and so, the 4. thereof, we came to our
Generall on the East shoare, and anchored in a fayre Harborough named Anne
Warrwickes sound, vnto whiche is an- The countesse of Warwick sound & Isle.
nexed an Islande both named after the
Countesse of Warrwicke, Anne Warrwickes sound and Isle.

In this Isle, our Generall thought Oure fraight surmounteth the charges of the first and second voyage, with suf ficient inte- rest to the ve turers.
good, for this voyage, to fraygbt both the
Ship and Barkes, with suche Stone or
Gold minerall, as he iudged to counter-
uaile the charges of his first, and this his
second Nauigation to these contries, w
sufficient interest to ŷ venturers, wherby they might bothe be satisfied for this

time

time, and alſo in time to come, (if it
pleaſe God and our Prince,) to erſpect
a much moze large benefite, out of the
bowells of thoſe Septentrionall Para-
lels, which long time hath concealed it
ſelf,til at this pzeſent,thzough the wonderfull diligence, & great danger of our
Generall and others, God is contented
with the reuealing thereof. It riſeth ſo
aboundantly, that from the beginning
of Auguſt,to the 22.thereof,(euery man
following the diligence of our General)
we rayſed aboue grounde 200. tunne,
whiche we iudged a reaſonable fraight
foz the Shippe and two Barkes, in the
ſayde Anne Warrwicks Iſle.

In the time of our abode here, ſome
of the countrie people, came to ſhewe
them ſelues vnto vs,ſundzie times on ye
maine ſhoare,nére adiacent to the ſayd
Iſle. Our Generall, deſirous to haue
ſome newes of his men, whome he loſt
the yeare befoze, with ſome companie
with him repaped with the Ship boat,
to common, oz ſigne with them foz familiaritie, wherevnto he is perſuaded
to

liches long
oncealed pre
ently diſco-
ered by cap-
eine Frobi-
her.

By Capteine
Frobiſhers di-
ligence other
men incoura-
ged to labor.

The countrie
people ſhewe
hem ſelues
nto vs.

The care
which our
General had
o heare of his
men that
vere loſt.

of Capteine Frobisher.

to bzing them. They, at the firſt ſhewe, made tokens, that thzẽ of his fiue men were aliue, and deſired penne, ynck, and paper, and that within thzẽ oz foure dayes, they would returne, and (as we iudged) bzing thoſe of our men, whiche were liuing, with them.

Signes for penne, yncke, and paper.

They alſo made ſignes oz tokens of their king, whom they called Cacough, and how he was carried on mens ſhoulders, and a man farre ſurmounting any of our companie, in bigneſſe and ſtature.

Cacough their King.

With theſe tokens and ſignes of wziting, penne, yncke, and paper was deliuered them, which they woulde not take at our handes: but being layde vpon the ſhoare, and the partie gone away, they tooke vp: which likewiſe they doe, when they deſire any thing foz chaunge of theirs, laying foz that which is left, ſo much as they think wil couteruaile the ſame, and not comming neare together. It ſẽmeth they haue bẽne vſed to this trade oz traffique, with ſome other people adioyning, oz not farre di-

Their vſage in traffique or exchange.

C.iij.   ſtant

ſtant from their Countrie.

The people ſhewe them ſelues againe on firme land.

After 4. dayes, ſome of them ſhewed themſelues vpon the firme land, but not where they were befoȝe. Our Generall, very glad thereof, ſuppoſing to heare of our men, went from the Iſlande, with the boate, and ſufficient companie with him.

Their craft to betray ſome of vs.

They ſéemed very glad, and allured him, about a certeine point of the land : behind which they might perceiue a companie of the craftie villains to lye lurking, whome our Generall woulde not deale withall, foȝ that he knewe not what companie they were, and ſo with fewe ſignes diſmiſſed them, and returned to his companie.

The people ſhewe them ſelues the third time.

An other time, as our ſaid Generall was coaſting the contrie, with two litle Pinniſſes, whereby at oure returne hée might make the better relation thereof, thȝée of the craftie villains, with a white ſkin allured vs to them. Once againe, our Generall, foȝ ẙ he hoped to heare of his men, went towardes them : at oure

A number of them hidden

comming néere the ſhoare, wheron they were, we might perceiue a number of them

of Capteine Frobisher.

them lie hidden behinde great stones, & those thrée in sight labouring by al meanes possible, that some woulde come on land: & perceyuing wée made no haste by wordes nor friendly signes, which they vsed by clapping of their handes, and béeing without weapon, and but thrée in sighte, they sought farther meanes to prouoke vs therevnto. One alone layd flesh on the shoare, whiche we toke vpp with the Boate hoke, as necessarie vitualls for the relieuing of the man, woman, & child, whom we had taken: for ý as yet, they could not digest oure meate: whereby they perceiued themselues deceiued of their expectation, for all their craftie allurements. Yet once againe, to make (as it were) a full shewe of their craftie natures, and subtile sleightes, to the intent thereby to haue intrapped and taken some of our men, one of them counterfeyted himselfe impotent and lame of his legges, who sémed to descend to the water side, with great difficultie: and to couer his crafte the more, one of his fellowes came downe with him

behind stones to betray vs.

Their firste meanes to allure vs to shoare.

Their second meanes.

Their thirde and craftiest allurement.

C.iiij.

him, and in such places, where he seemed vnable to passe; hee tooke him on his shoulders, set him by the water side, and

craftie coun-
set villaine.

departed from him, leauing him (as it should seeme) all alone, who playing his counterfeite pageant very well, thought thereby to prouoke some of vs to come on shoare, not fearing, but that any one of vs might make oure partie good with a lame man.

Our Generall, hauing compassion

compassion
cure a craf-
e lame man.

of his impotencie, thought good (if it were possible) to cure him therof: wherfore, hee caused a souldiour to shoote at him with his Caleeuer, which grased before his face. The counterfeite villeine deliuerly fled, without any impediment at all, and gott him to his bowe and arrowes, and the rest from their lurking holes, with their weapons, bowes, arrowes, slings, and dartes. Our Generall caused some Caleeuers to be shet off

some hurt
with our shot.

at them, whereby some being hurt, they mighte hereafter stand in more feare of vs.

This was all the aunswere, for this time,

of *Capteine Frobisher.*

tion, wee could haue of our men, or of
our Generals letter. Their craftie dea-
ling, at these three seuerall times, being
thus manifest vnto vs, maye plainely
shewe their disposition in other thinges
to be correspondent. We iudged, that
they vsed these stratagemmes, thereby
to haue caught some of vs, for the deliue-
ring of the man, woman, & child whome
we haue taken.

By these craf-
tie trickes the
rest of their
life is easy to
be iudged.

They are men of a large corpora-
ture, and good proportion : their colour
is not much vnlike the Sunne burnte
Countrie man, who laboureth daily in
the Sunne for his liuing.

Their stature
and makin

They weare their haire somethinge
long, and cut before, either with stone or
knife, very disorderly. Their women
weare their haire long, and knit vp with
two loupes, shewing forth on either side
of their faces, and the rest foltred vp on
a knot. Also, some of their women race
their faces proportionally, as chinne,
cheekes, and forehead, and the wristes of
their handes, wherevpon they lay a colour, which continueth darke azurine.

Their appa
as wel wom
as men.

C.b.　　　They

They eate their meate all rawe, both fleshe, fishe, and foule, or something per-boyled with bloud & a little water, which they drinke. For lacke of water, they wil eate yce, that is hard frosen, as plea-santly as we will doe Sugar Candie, or other Sugar.

If they, for necessities sake, stand in néede of the premisses, such grasse as the countrie yéeldeth they plucke vppe, and eate, not deintily, or salletwise, to allure their stomaches to appetite : but for ne-cessities sake, without either salt, oyles, or washing, like brutish beasts deuoure the same. They neither vse table, stoole, or table cloth for comelinesse : but when they are imbrued with bloud, knuckle déepe, and their kniues in like sort, they vse their tongues as apt instruments to licke them cleane : in doeing whereof, they are assured to lose none of their victuals.

They franck or kéep certeine doggs, not much vnlike Wolues, whiche they yoke together, as we do oxen and horses, to a sled or traile : and so carrie their ne-cessaries

(marginal notes:) ir meate, ke, and o- necessa-

y eate the se whiche weth in countrie.

barous be-iour.

gges like o wolues,

cessaries ouer the yce and snowe, from place to place : as the captiue, whom we haue, made perfecte signes . And when those Dogges are not apt for the same vse : or when with hunger they are con- streyned, for lacke of other victuals, they eate them : so that they are as needefull for them , in respect of their bignesse , as our oren are for vs.

They eate dogges flesh

They apparell themselues in the skinnes of such beastes as they kill, se- wed together with the sinewes of them. All the fowle which they kill , they skin, and make thereof one kinde of garment or other, to defend them from the cold.

Sinewes of beasts serue them in place of thread.

They make their apparell with hoods and tailes, which tailes they giue, when they thinke to gratifie any friendshippe shewed vnto them : a great signe of friendshippe with them. The men haue them not so syde as the women.

Hoodes and tailes to their apparell.

The men and women weare their hose close to their legges, from the wast to the knee, without any open before, as well the one kinde as the other. Uppon their legges , they weare hose of lether, with

Their hose and how they are worne

with the furre side inward, two oz thzée paire on at once, and especially the women. In those hose, they put their knues, néedles, and other thinges néedefull to beare about. They put a bone within their hose, whiche reacheth from the foote to the knée, whereupon they dzawe their said hose, and so in place of garters, they are holden from falling downe about their féete.

They dzesse their skinnes very softe and souple with the haire on. In cold weather oz Winter, they weare ý furre side inward: and in Summer outward. Other apparell they haue none, but the said skinnes.

Those beastes, flesh, fishes, and fowles, which they kil, they are both meate, dzinke, apparel, houses, bedding, hose, shoes, thzed, saile foz their boates, with many other necessaries, whereof they stande in néede, and almost all their riches.

Their houses are tentes, made of Seale skinns, pitched with foure Firre quarters, foure square, méeting at the toppe,

(marginal notes) ir garte- ... ir chiefe ...s. ... r houses ale skin- nd Firre.

toppe, and the ſkinnes ſewed together
with ſinowes, and layd therevppon : ſo
pitched they are, that the entraunce into them, is alwayes South , oʒ againſt
the Sunne.

They haue other ſoʒtes of houſes,
whiche wæ found, not to be inhabited,
which are raiſed with ſtones and Whal
bones, and a ſkinne layd ouer them, to
withſtand the raine , oʒ other weather:
the entraunce of them béeing not much
vnlike an Ouens mouth, whereto, I
thincke, they reſoʒt foʒ a time, to fiſhe,
hunt, and fowle, and ſo leaue them foʒ
the next time they come thether againe.

Their weapons are Bowes , Arrowes, Dartes, and Slinges. Their
Bowes are of a yard long of wod, ſi-
newed on the back with ſtrong veines,
not glued to, but faſt girded and tyed
on. Their Bowe ſtringes are likewiſe
ſinewes. Their arrowes are thʒée pée-
ces, nocked with bone, and ended with
bone, with thoſe two ends, and the wod
in the middſt, they paſſe not in lengthe
halfe a yard oʒ little moʒe. They are fe-
                                        thered

Their wea-
pons of de-
fence.

thered with two fethers, the penne end
being cutte away, and the fethers layd
vppon the arrowe with the broad ſide to
the woode: in ſomuch that they ſéeme,
when they are tyed on, to haue foure fethers. They haue likewiſe thré ſortes
of heades to thoſe arrowes: one ſort of
ſtone or yron, proportioned like to a
heart: the ſecond ſort of bone, much like
vnto a ſtopte head, with a hooke on the
ſame: the thirde ſort of bone likewiſe,
made ſharpe at both ſides, and ſharpe
pointed. They are not made very faſt,
but lightly tyed to, or elſe ſet in a nocke,
that vppon ſmall occaſion, the arrowe
leaueth theſe heades behinde them: and
they are of ſmall force, except they be very néere, when they ſhoote.

Their Darts are made of two ſorts:
the one with many forkes of bone in
the fore ende, and likewiſe in the mid-
deſt: their proportions are not muche
vnlike our toaſting yrons, but longer:
theſe they caſt out of an inſtrument of
wood, very readily. The other ſorte is
greater then the firſt aforeſayde, with a
                                        long

(marginal notes:) e ſortes ades to arrowes.

ſortes of s.

long bone made sharp on both sides, not much vnlike a Rapier, which I take to be their most hurtfull weapon.

They haue two sorts of boates, made of Lether, set out on the inner side with quarters of wood, artificially tyed together with thongs of the same: the greater sort are not much vnlike our Wherries, wherein sixtéene or twentie men may sitte: they haue for a sayle, or est the guttes of such beastes as they kyll, very fine and thinne, which they sewe together: the other boate is but for one man to sitte and rowe in, with one oare.

Two sortes of
Boates made
of Leather.

Their order of fishing, hunting, and fowling, are with these sayde weapons: but in what sort, or how they vse them, we haue no perfect knowledge as yet.

They vse to
fowle, fish, &
hunt.

I can not suppose their abode or habitation to be here, for that neither their houses, or apparell, are of no such force to withstand the extremitie of colde, that the countrie séemeth to be infected withall: neyther doe I sée any signe likely to performe the same.

It is to be
supposed th
their inhabi
ting is else-
where.

Those houses, or rather dennes,
which

which ſtand there, haue no ſigne of foot=
way, oʒ any thing elſe troden, whiche is
one of the chiefeſt tokens of habitation.
And thoſe tents, which they bʒing with

eir tentes
=moueable
m place to
ce.

them, when they haue ſufficiently hun=
ted and fiſhed, they remoue to other
places: and when they haue ſufficient=
ly ſtoʒed them of ſuche victuals, as the
countrie yeldeth, oʒ bʒingeth foʒth, they
returne to their Winter ſtations oʒ ha=
bitations. This coniecture do J make,
foʒ the infertilitie, whiche J perceiue to
be in that countrie.

heir vſe of
on.

They haue ſome yʒon, whereof they
make arrowe heades, kniues, and other
little inſtrumentes, to woʒke their boa=
tes, bowes, arrowes, and dartes withal,
whiche are very vnapt to doe any thing
withall, but with great labour.

It ſæmeth, that they haue conuerſa=
tion with ſome other people, of whome,
foʒ erchaunge, they ſhould receiue the
ſame. They are greatly delighted with

Vherin they
light.

any thinge that is bʒighte, oʒ giueth a
ſound.

What knowledge they haue of God,
oʒ what

oʒ what ʃool they adoʒe, wée haue no
perfect intelligence. I thincke them rather Anthropophagi, oʒ deuourers of
mans fleʃhe, then otherwiʃe: foʒ that
there is no fleʃh oʒ fiʃhe, which they finde
dead, (ʃmell it neuer ʃo filthily) but they
will eate it, as they finde it, without any
other dʒeʃʃing. A loathʃome ʃpectacle, either to the beholders, oʒ hearers.

*Anthropo-
phagi.*

*A filthie fe-
ding.*

*A loathʃome
ʃpectacle.*

　There is no maner of cʒéeping beaʃt
hurtful, except ʃome Spiders (which, as
many affirme, are ʃignes of great ʃtoʒe
of Golde:) and alʃo certeine ʃtinging
Gnattes, which bite ʃo fiercely, that the
place where they bite, ʃhoʒtly after
ʃwelleth, and itcheth very ʃoʒe.

*Signes of go-
aure.*

*Stinging
Gnattes.*

　They make ʃignes of certeine people, that weare bʒight plates of Gold in
their foʒheads, and other places of their
bodies.

*Signes of g-
from other
people.*

　The Countries, on both ʃides the
ʃtreightes, lye very highe with roughe
ʃtonie mounteynes, and great quantitie
of ʃnowe thereon. There is very little
plaine ground, and no graʃʃe, except a litle, whiche is much like vnto moʃʃe that

*Deʃcriptio
of the coun-
tries.*

*No graʃʃe,
like moʃʃe.*

　　　　　Ɗ.　　　　　groweth

Countrie
hat yeeldeth
othing with
oote, fitt for
he vſe of
Man.

eere with
kinnes like
Aſſes:

ares, Wol-
s, & fiſhing
ares:

figne of
rthquakes
thunder.

groweth on ſoft ground, ſuch as we gett
Turfes in. There is no wood at all. To
be briefe, there is nothing fitte, or profi-
table for ẙ vſe of man, which that Countrie with roote ẙeldeth, or bringeth forth:
Howbeit, there is great quantitie of
Deere, whoſe ſkinnes are like vnto
Aſſes, their heads or hornes doe farre ex-
ceed, as wel in length as alſo in breadth,
any in theſe oure partes or Countrie:
their feete likewiſe, are as great as oure
oxens, whiche we meaſured to be ſeuen
or eight ynches in breadth. There are
alſo Hares, Wolues, fiſhing-Beares,
and Sea foule of ſundrie ſortes.

As the Countrie is barren and vn-
fertile, ſo are they rude and of no capa-
citie to culture the ſame, to any perfec-
tion: but are contented by their hunting, fiſhing, and fowling, with rawe
fleſh and warme bloud, to ſatiſfie their
greedie panches, whiche is their only
glorie.

There is great likelyhood of Earth-
quakes, or thunder: for that huge and
monſtruous mounteynes, whoſe grea-
teſt

test substaunce are stones, and those sto=
nes so shaken with some extraordinarie
meanes, that one is separated from ano=
ther, whiche is discordant from all other
Quarries.

There are no riuers, or running
springes, but such, as through the heate
of the Sunne, with such water as des=
cendeth from the mounteines and hills,
whereon great driftes of snowe doe lie,
are ingendred.

It argueth also, that there should be
none: for that the earth, whiche with the
extremitie of the Winter, is so frosen
within, that that water, whiche should
haue recourse within the same, to main=
teine Springes, hath not his motion,
whereof great waters haue their origi=
nall, as by experience is seene other=
where. Such valleies, as are capable to
receiue the water, that in the Summer
time, by the operation of the Sunne, des=
cendeth from great abundance of snow,
whiche continually lyeth on the moun=
teines, and hath no passage, sinketh into
the earth, and so banisheth awaye, with=

No riuers, but such as the Sunne doeth cause to come of snowe.

A probabili= tie, that the should be n ther spring riuers in the ground.

Springes th original of great waters

D.ij.   out

out any runnell aboue the earth , by which occasion, oz continual standing of the said water , the earth is opened, and the great frost yeldeth to the force thereof, whiche in other places , foure oz fiue fathoms within the ground, foz lacke of the said moysture, (ths earth, euen in the very Summer time,) is frosen, and so combineth the stones together , that scarcely instruments, with great force, can vnknitte them.

he stones
ofen within
ic earth 4.oz
fathoms.

Also , where the water in those ballies can haue no such passage away , by the continuaunce of time, in such ozder as is befoze rehearsed, the yearely descent from the mounteines , filleth them ful, that at the lowest banck of the same, they fall into the next vallie, and so continue, as fishing Pondes oz Stagnes in the Summer time full of water, and in the Winter hard frosen : as by skarres that remaine thereof in Summer, may easily be perceiued : so that, the heate of Summer, is nothing comparable, oz of force, to dissolue the extremitie of colde, that commeth in Winter.

he heate in
immer not
mparable
the cold in
iuter.

Neuer

of Capteine Frobisher.

Neuerthelesse, I am assured, that be-
lowe the force of the frost, within the
earth, the waters haue recourse, and
emptie themselues out of sighte into the
sea, which through the extremitie of the
frost, are constreyned to doe the same, by
which occasion, the earth within is kept
the warmer, and springes haue their recourse, which is the onely nutriment of
Gold and Minerals within the same.

There is much to be said of the commodities of these Countries, which are
couched within the bowels of the earth,
which I let passe till more perfect triall
be made thereof.

Thus coniecturing, till time, with the
earnest industrie of our Generall and o-
thers (who by al diligence remaine prest
to explore the truth of that which is vn-
explored, as he hath to his euerlasting
praise found out that whiche is like to
yælde an innumerable benefite to his
Prince & countrie:) offer further triall,
I conclude.

The 23. of August, after wée had satisfied our mindes with fraybht sufficient,

Springes vn-
der the force
of the frost
within the
earth.

The earth b
occasion of
frost kept t
warmer.

Springs no
rish gold.

An end of c
iecturing ti
further tru
and triall.

Shippes sa
fied with b
then, but

ns mindes
t contented.

ent for oure veſſels, though not our coueteous deſires, with ſuch knowledge of the countrie people and other commodities as are before rehearſed, the 24. therof wée departed therehence: the 17. of September we fell with ý lands end of England, and ſo to Milford hauen, from whence our General rode to the Court, for order, to what port or hauen to conduct the ſhippe.

r departure
m theſe
untries.

We loſt our two Barkes in the way homeward, the one, the 29. of Auguſt, the other, the 31. of the ſame moneth; by occaſion of great tempeſt and fogge. Howbeit, God reſtored the one to Briſtowe, and ý other making his courſe by Scotland to Yermouth. In this voyage wée loſt two men, one in the waye by Gods viſitation, and the other homewarde caſt ouer borde with a ſurge of the ſea.

we, and
en, we loſt
r 2. Barks,
ich God
nertheleſſe
ored.

I Could declare vnto your Honour, the Latitude and Longitude of ſuch places and regions, as wée haue béene at, but not altogether ſo perfect as our maiſters and others, with many circumſtances

e concluſi-

of Capteine Frobisher.

ſtances of tempeſts and other accidents
incident to ſea faring men, which ſæme
not altogether ſtraunge, I let paſſe to
their repoztes as men moſt apte to ſett
fozth and declare the ſame. I haue alſo
left the names of the countries on both
the ſhoares vntouched, foz lacke of vn-
derſtanding the Peoples language: as
alſo foz ſundzie reſpectes, not nædfull as
yet to be declared.

Countries new explozed, where commoditie is to be loked foz, doe better ac-
cozd with a new name giuen by the ex-
plozers, then an vncerteine name by a
doubtfull Authour.

Dur General named ſundzie Iſlands,
Mounteines, Capes, and Harbozoughs
after the names of diuers Noble men,
and other gentlemen his friends, as wel
on the one ſhoare, as alſo on the other:
not fozgetting amongeſt the reſte your
Lozdſhip: whiche hereafter (when
occaſion ſerueth) are to be declared in his own Mapps
oz Charts.

FINIS.

www.ingramcontent.com/pod-product-compliance
Lightning Source LLC
Chambersburg PA
CBHW031931060726
47496CB00008BA/2865